THE NANNY
THE FAMILY HEL

Published by Julie Day
Copyright 2018 Julie Day
Cover by Joleene Naylor

This ebook is licensed for your personal enjoyment only. This ebook may not be resold or given away to other people. If you would like to share this book with another person, please purchase an additional copy for each recipient. If you're reading this book and did not purchase it, or it was not purchased for your use only, then please return to the retailer where you bought it and purchase your own copy. Thank you for respecting the hard work of this author.

"Will you two stop running around before one of you falls and hurts yourself!"

I'd been hoping for a few minutes' peace after our meal.

Too late. Jenny crashed to the floor and there was a cry of, "Mum, Sam tripped me up."

"No, I didn't!" Sam shouted.

"That's enough, you two," I said. "Tim, could you please deal with Jenny?" I asked the top of my husband's head.

"Quieten it," he ordered from behind the newspaper.

Silence.

I sighed. That was better, but would it last?

But then, hardly had the question entered my head than five-month-old Robbie cried so shrilly that I thought the glass in the cabinet would crack.

"Oh no. Not joining in, too, are you, Robbie?"

Sam stuck his leg out as Jenny went past him.

"Sam, stop that," I told him, wagging a finger. "That's not nice. You're six. She's only four. You should know better. Say sorry to your sister."

"Sorry," he mumbled, and stuck his tongue out.

How would I get on with work and the children when they were at home all day on holiday? I had an idea. "Tim, do you think that we could hire a nanny to keep an eye on the children? I think we can afford it. I'll never get this commission done while ever they are behaving like this."

He put the paper down and looked at me. "How long for?" he asked.

"Just for this next week. I'm sure I recall Florence next door mentioning that her daughter is a trained nanny, so perhaps I could ask her."

"Might be good for them to listen to someone else. Perhaps they will behave better."

"Exactly," I said. "Will you keep an eye on them while I pop next door?"

"Now?"

"Why not, while I'm thinking about it."

I left Tim to it.

I rang the bell. After a few minutes, Florence answered.

"Hello," I said. "Oh, have you got visitors?" I could hear a voice inside.

"Yes, my daughter, Sally. She's here for a few days."

"Is it possible I can come in to talk to her? I need her help."

"With the children?"

"Ah, you've heard their noise. I do apologise."

Inside I met Sally. "Hello," I said, "I live next door."

"The mother of the three children?"

"Yes. I know you can hear them. They're awfully noisy. That's why I'm here. Your mother once told me you are a trained nanny and I could really do with somebody like you now. My husband is out working and I have a design website to run, and I'm finding it hard looking after the children while they're at home during the holiday. I was wondering, would you be able to help?"

"I'm sorry," she replied, "I work full-time for a family across town. I tell you what I'll do, though: I will spread the word around the other nannies I know. You could try the agency, of course."

Back home, Sam and Jenny were still running around the house, shrieking.

"Any luck?" Tim asked.

"No. She's got a full-time job, but she's going to ask some of her contacts. She did suggest asking the agency she works with as well."

Ten minutes later, while I was struggling to feed Robbie, and with the kids still running riot – I didn't know where they got the energy – and Tim sitting with his laptop on his knees, the doorbell rang.

"Who's that now?" I ran my fingers through my hair, pulling off my hair band. "Could you get that, Tim, while I feed Robbie?"

But Robbie wailed louder as I offered him a spoonful of food. "On the other hand," I said, "you feed Robbie. I'll answer the door."

On the doorstep stood a young girl dressed in a silver blouse that glimmered in the light, black trousers with knife-sharp creases and slip-on shoes that gleamed as if they were brand new.

"I heard that you might need a nanny for a short time," she said, "and thought I could help."

"Oh, that was quick. I didn't expect to hear so soon. Do come in."

"Stop that, you two. Now!" Tim shouted, creating even more noise. If he couldn't get them to behave, could this slip of a girl?

"If you heard that," I said, slightly embarrassed, "then you'll know what we have to put up with. Do you think you could do any better? They seem to be unmanageable sometimes."

"You don't know what I can do," she said.

That seemed a strange thing to say, but as she spoke she smiled, and as she did, I felt a sense of the world being right come over me.

"OK, then, let's give it a try. Come on in." I stood aside for her.

As she stepped into the hall, I smelt a faint hint of lavender. When she moved, she glided as if she was on ice.

The noise of the children arguing became louder and louder. Tim hadn't had much success getting them to be quiet. What could this young girl do that we couldn't? Would she live up to her claim?

In the dining room, Sam and Jenny ran about yelling at each other. Tim had given up on feeding Robbie and the gloop was running down Robbie's chin.

Taking all this in, the girl stood with her arms crossed. "What's this noise?" she asked quietly.

At the sound of a strange voice the children stood still. And it was strange. It was like a gentle whisper of comfort and calm.

Wow! They never do that for me.

"That's more like it. Now, go and wash your hands, and come back down ... quietly," she told them.

To my amazement, Sam and Jenny did as they were told. They even came back quietly. How could someone so petite – five foot at most – have such a controlled and calming presence? It certainly had an effect.

Then I realised we hadn't had time to introduce ourselves properly. What with the stress I was under when she first arrived and being so taken aback by the way she had calmed the children, I hadn't thought to ask her name.

"Tim, this is ..." I began, glancing at her questioningly.

"Victoria Harris, but everyone calls me Vicky. I've moved in next door for a bit, and heard that you needed a nanny. I trained as one."

She must mean on the other side of our terrace, I thought fleetingly, otherwise Florence or Sally would have mentioned her. But I didn't have time to dwell on that at that moment.

"I'm Penny Jameson and this is my husband, Tim. You're right, Vicky, we do need help. No matter how many times I tell them to be quiet, they won't shut up," I admitted. "They seem to go on and on. They never let up." My shoulders drooped. "I wish I could have some me time."

Robbie gave a cry.

Vicky went to him and, bending down, cooed, "And who's this handsome little fella?"

"That's Robbie. He's five months old," I said.

"Hello, Robbie. I'm Vicky." Seeing the blobs and stains on his bib, she said, "Don't you like your dinner? Why's that?" and she ate a spoonful herself.

For the first time since Vicky's arrival, Tim had taken proper notice of her. He said, "Is that hygienic, eating from the same spoon?"

"If it works, then let her do it," I said. "I've tried that, but he still hates it."

"Mmmm. This is yummy," Vicky said, moving her mouth up and down as if she was eating. "I can't see what's wrong with it. Go on, have a taste." She fed another spoonful to Robbie. He spat it out. Maybe she wasn't that good after all. But I hadn't bargained for her determination.

"Stubborn, are we? Want me to eat it all myself, do you? That's not fair. We'll go halves."

She ate another mouthful, licked her lips extravagantly, then gave him another spoonful. It worked; Robbie actually swallowed a whole mouthful without spitting any of it out.

Tim and I looked on in disbelief as Robbie ate his whole dinner.

"Well, I never. He's not done that for me. I end up getting it everywhere but in his mouth. How did you do that? What did you do? Put a magic spell on it?"

Vicky looked up at me and smiled, and it felt as though the day was getting sunnier and the stress was being eased out of my body.

"You just need to show him you like it, too. And no nose-wriggling! He can pick up on that and refuse it," she told me.

I laughed. That was exactly what I did when I gave Robbie his food. How did she know this?

Vicky wiped Robbie's mouth, and said, "If you want to go out, I'm happy to stay and babysit. I know we've only just met, but as I am next door ..."

I glanced at Tim. "Shall we? You so often come home to noise and me frazzled," I said.

"Are you sure you'll able to cope, Vicky?" I asked. "They can be a handful."

"We'll be fine," she said.

Tim frowned, thinking. "The kids seem to like and trust her," he said eventually, "so I think we should too."

I was sure that the smell of lavender had become stronger. It was calming and I felt my muscles relax and an energy buzz through my body.

"Thank you, Vicky. We'll take you up on your offer," Tim said.

In the restaurant, the quiet atmosphere gave me time to think about Vicky, and how she had managed to calm the children, especially for someone so young and petite.

"How do you think she manages to keep the kids so quiet, when she isn't that old and she's so small? She looks as if a gust of wind would knock her over."

"She is a trained nanny," he replied, "so must have the knowledge and tricks to tame them."

"I suppose." Then a flower on our table reminded me of her perfume.

"Did you smell lavender when she was near you?" I remembered how the scent had affected me.

"Now you mention it, yes, I did smell lavender."

"You did, too? How did you feel when you smelt it?"

He stared at me as though I was the one who was strange.

"What are you getting at?" he asked.

"You haven't answered my question."

"OK. When I smelt lavender, I felt …" He paused.

"Well?"

"I felt calm and happy," he said.

"So did I. What's happening, Tim? Who is this Vicky Harris?"

"I say, let it go for now. Just relax and be happy she can control the kids."

Maybe Tim was right. It was great that Vicky could manage the children; we should just be glad that she could do it. But there was something niggling at the back of my mind: there was something odd about Vicky, which I couldn't put my finger on.

Our starters came then and I put thoughts of Vicky to one side.

That was, until we got back to the house, and to quiet.

I looked at Tim, and he shrugged.

"Where do you think they are?" I asked him.

"In bed?"

"So quickly? If they are, then Vicky is a miracle worker. Either that or she has put a magic spell on them." I did wonder, thinking about the effect of the lavender scent on me.

I went upstairs.

I stepped into Sam's room first. It was in darkness and quiet, except for the whisper of a faint grunt under the sheets. Yes, there was the familiar lump of his body in bed, hugging his bear, Ted, his favourite toy, which he wouldn't go to sleep without, but hated being told about this.

Content he was deep in his slumber, I went into Jenny's room, where in the dimness I saw Vicky sitting on the bedside chair.

Hearing the door open, she turned around. "Shhh. They're fast asleep," she whispered. "I don't want to wake them up."

I nodded to indicate I understood all too well. If you woke Jenny it'd take hours to get her back to sleep. But being a mother, I tiptoed forward and leant over the bed.

Yes, she, too, was sound asleep, and, like Sam, hugging her favourite toy, Lucy, her dolly.

I whispered to Vicky, "Thank you," before backing out of the door and returning to Tim in the living room.

"They're both sound asleep," I told him.

"There you are. I told you we could trust Vicky."

I caught a whiff of lavender then and, turning round, I came face to face with Vicky. Where had she appeared from? I hadn't heard her come down the stairs or heard the door behind me creak open as it normally did.

"Thank you again for looking after them and getting them to bed," I said, my doubts forgotten. "How much do we owe you?"

"I will ask the … agency," she replied. "I'll see myself out."

I was so bound up in being in a quiet house for once that it didn't sink in that I hadn't heard Vicky go out of the front door, or heard any door shut.

In bed, Vicky was our main subject of conversation.

"It's quiet next door, isn't it? I thought young people liked loud music," Tim said.

"Perhaps she just wants some peace after looking after Sam and Jenny. I know I would."

"Guess you're right."

I closed my eyes and tried to forget about the strange events of the day.

* * *

Until the Monday morning when Vicky appeared at the front door. I stared at the gate. I hadn't heard it squeak as it usually did whenever anyone opened it. Had she put a spell on that, too?

In the living room, she said, "Good morning, Sam and Jenny."

They stopped hitting each other and turned round to face her. Sam said, "Hi, Vicky," then Jenny said, "Hi," both quietly instead of yelling.

And so it continued.

When Vicky told Sam to pick up his toys after he'd finished playing with them, he walked over to them, picked them up and put them in the box. Would Jenny do the same? I willed her to misbehave, just to see how Vicky handled it.

She tried her luck, taking out a toy from the box and chucking it on to the floor.

Vicky said in her quiet way, "Jenny, pick that up, please, and put it back into the box where you got it from."

"Blimey!" I whispered, as Jenny slowly picked up the toy and dropped it back into its box.

"Thank you, Jenny. Good girl," Vicky told her.

They never obey me like that.

It seemed as if a voice had gone into their heads telling them they had to do as they were told.

"Thank you, Vicky. You are a miracle worker," I said.

* * *

"You just need to speak quietly and to show them you are in charge, not yell at them," she said the next morning.

"Is that all there is to it?"

"No, it can be about the way you dress as well."

"What's wrong with my clothes?" I asked, glancing down at my jeans and T-shirt with a huge daisy on it.

"I think that Sam and Jenny see you more as a friendly mother than a mother who is in control. If you dress like you're in authority to them, then they might get the message that you are the one in charge, not them."

"I tend to wear these for feeding Robbie."

"Yes, you can wear those for that, but then change into something more formal, as if you were going to work."

I could see what she meant. The children *were* work, indeed. I thought about what Vicky had been wearing: flares and a blouse, which looked feminine and authoritative at the same time. Was that part of her magic? If so, if it worked for her, then I'd give it a go.

I changed into a pair of grey trousers and a red blouse. Red for power, I mused.

Downstairs, I asked Tim, who was going into work later that day. "Do you think I look like a mum in charge now?"

"Wow! You look like you mean business! Yes, darling, you do look like you're in charge. I think I'll stay out of your way!"

Then I noticed his eyes wander to my cleavage and a smile lit up his face. I laughed. He hadn't done that in a while, either.

"Good, just the image I wanted to portray to the children. Make them take notice of me." Like you did, I thought.

Vicky appeared then, where from I didn't know because I hadn't heard her approach. "How do I look now?" I asked her.

"That is good. Much better," she replied. "You can be in charge now." She laughed, a soft gentle sound.

It was as if the sun had come out to shine on me, and I could do anything I wanted.

I wasn't the only thing the sun had shone on. I was sure the flowers on the wallpaper had a blue shadow to them. I shook my head. I felt strange – powerful. With this new feeling of power, I said to her, "I don't think I need you for the rest of the day, Vicky, so you can have some time for yourself. You must have things to do. Oh, did you get to speak to your agency about fees?"

"I will ask," she replied.

"Oh, and I suppose I should have references, too."

"I will ask," she repeated.

Intrigued by the quiet girl who could calm my wayward children, I went to follow her out of the living room door to see where she went, but I blinked, and in that moment, when I opened my eyes, she had disappeared. Where had she gone? I hadn't heard a door shut.

"What's wrong?" Tim asked, coming into the room.

"Did you hear a door shut just then?"

"No."

"Vicky has gone home. One minute she was there in front of me, the next she wasn't. And I didn't hear a thing."

"Maybe she shut the door carefully so as not to disturb the children now that they're behaving themselves."

"Perhaps."

Meanwhile, I wanted to find out how Vicky managed to make Sam and Jenny so quiet and obedient all the time. I needed to get her on her own. And there was that niggling feeling I had about her that I wanted to get to the bottom of.

"I'm off to work now," Tim said. "Be good," he called out to the children.

Without Vicky and their dad, would they behave? Could I get on with some work?

Leaving them quietly playing with their toys, I went upstairs with Robbie. I put him in his playpen, while I went on to my computer. I left the door open just in case.

After half an hour there was still silence. I saved the alterations I had made to the design I was working on, and went to the door. Robbie had dozed off. Then I tiptoed down to the living room and peeped round the door. Sam and Jenny were sitting on the floor playing cards. That was a first. No sign of Vicky, but they were acting as if she was there, standing over them. I could still smell that lavender scent, so perhaps they could sense her, too.

* * *

The rest of the week passed in the same way, with the children being quiet and obedient, and not just when Vicky was in the house. I'd never known a half-term like it, not since Sam started school.

On the Friday morning I managed to get Vicky alone on the landing. Tim was in the bedroom getting ready for work, and Sam and Jenny were just waking up.

I asked her, "Vicky, I've often watched you with the children and marvelled at how they obey you. I wish I could be like that. Have you a magic spell or something?"

"No, it's nothing mystical. You've got to be fair and authoritative at the same time. If that doesn't work, then blackmail helps."

"Blackmail? That's a bit harsh, isn't it?"

"Depends on how you put it. Take Jenny, for instance. She likes her bedtime story. So if she won't go to bed then say to her if she doesn't, she won't get read to. Why don't you try it? Try it tomorrow if she's difficult at bedtime and see what reaction you get. Another trick is to think about what your parents did to get you to behave at their age."

As she spoke to me, I felt a mist of calm surround me, and I immediately knew I could do what she had suggested. "Thanks, Vicky. I might just try that."

And for the first time I saw her face properly and noticed her eyes. They were blank, as though she was looking straight through me. They were in contrast to the rest of her face: the dimple in her chin and her small, stubby nose, which made her look younger than she probably was, and gave her a cheery look, especially when she smiled. Those eyes were grave and serious compared with her cheery face and disposition.

I felt my heart start racing as something occurred to me – I was sure I'd seen those facial features somewhere before. But where? And on whom? Who was this girl with blank eyes? Where had she come from? Although she was strange, she did talk sense.

I thought about the blackmail idea for the rest of the day and decided to give it a go, if necessary.

* * *

So the next night I waited until the children's bedtime. Vicky had left and Tim had only just got in and I thought that if Sam and Jenny played up I'd try it on my own to see what happened.

As expected, Sam and Jenny ran about in and out of their bedrooms and along the landing, refusing to get into bed. Though annoying, it was the perfect opportunity.

"Where's Vicky?" Sam asked, pouting.

"She's gone home," I told him.

He jumped up and down, then ran around and around. Unfortunately, Jenny saw him and joined in.

Taking a deep breath, I told Jenny in a clear voice, "Right, young lady, if you don't get into bed this minute, I won't read you your story."

"Daddy or Vicky will," she retaliated. She crossed her arms over her body in her you-can't-make-me stance.

"Oh no, they won't. Vicky's not here, and I'll tell Daddy not to. What's it to be?" I watched her, defying her to answer back, standing straight with my arms crossed like hers were. Two can play at that game, I silently told her.

A few seconds later, Jenny trudged into her bedroom and jumped into bed.

"There's a good girl. I'll be in in a minute."

I looked at Sam, eyebrows raised. What could I say that would make him get into his room? What did he like most? His sugary breakfast.

"And you, Sam, if you don't get into bed this minute, you won't get your Coco Pops for breakfast. Instead you can have Weetabix, like your sister."

"Ugh. No way. I'm going."

I smiled as Sam stormed into his bedroom.

He was about to slam his door shut behind him, but I calmly told him, like Vicky would have done, "Don't slam the door on me." He shut it with a determined loud click instead. I punched the air. Yes! It had worked. Thank you, Vicky.

Back downstairs, Tim was waiting for me. And with him was Vicky. Eh! When did she appear? I hadn't heard her. Mind you, with the kids' noise it would've been hard to hear anything else.

"Well, I did what you suggested and it worked wonderfully. Thank you, Vicky."

She smiled and a sense of achievement came over me. Out of the corner of my eye I was sure I saw the walls take on a blue tint. Then they shone, and the dirty marks that had been there before all disappeared and everything looked clean. I coughed. I covered my mouth with my hand, taking my eye off Vicky for a moment. And when I looked up again, she had gone.

"Where did she go?" I blurted out. "I wanted to ask her about the fees. I feel we owe her so much now."

"Home," Tim said.

Where was home? She'd said next door. She couldn't live there, surely, because ... old Mrs Harris did, and had done for years.

Mrs Harris ... Harris. The name rang a bell. "Tim, what did Vicky say her surname was?"

"Harris," he replied.

"Oh my," I muttered.

"What's up?"

"Who lives next door?"

"Old Mrs ... Harris," he said, light beginning to dawn.

"You don't think they're related, do you?" I asked.

I pictured Mrs Harris and Vicky. And I gasped. I knew there was something familiar about her. That was where I'd seen the chin dimple and small nose before – Mrs Harris. Exactly the same, in the same place.

"Tim, make sure the kids don't wake up. I'm going to visit Mrs Harris. I have a weird feeling about this."

I strode out of the house, leaving Tim standing there looking bemused.

The more I thought about it, the more unnerved and jittery I became. I wanted to hear what Mrs Harris said, although I had a feeling deep down that I wouldn't like it. I had to get to the truth, no matter what it was.

Standing outside Mrs Harris's front door, I took a deep breath. I hoped I wasn't waking her up.

Slowly, I raised my hand and pressed the bell.

After a minute I heard a shuffling coming towards the door. Then it opened and Mrs Harris was standing there – smiling at me. Had she expected me? No, she couldn't have.

"Hello, Mrs Harris. I hope I'm not disturbing you this time of night, but I wanted to ask you something."

"No, you're not disturbing me, dear. Come on in," she said, leading the way to her living room.

Immediately I saw photos of people all around the room. One in particular caught my eye. As if drawn to it, I walked towards it.

"Mrs Harris, who is this?" I asked, although I had already guessed. I wanted to hear her say it out loud.

"That is my granddaughter, Vicky, or was," she said.

"Was?" I asked. It came out a squeak.

"Yes. She sadly died a few years ago. Drugs, I'm afraid."

Then Mrs Harris said, "Sometimes I think I can smell lavender. Vicky loved to wear that scent."

I shivered.

"Mrs Harris, do you have any other photos of Vicky?"

"Oh yes. Wait there and I'll get you some more."

While I waited, I looked around the room, and for the first time noticed the wallpaper. The walls were a sky blue, the same colour as ours had gone when Vicky smiled. I heard her coming back and she appeared with a photo album. I could see it was old from the yellow edges and it rustled crisply as she turned a page over.

She flipped over page after page, and as each page was turned, I could hear my heart beat louder with it. I dreaded what I was going to see, even though I knew what it would be.

"Ah, here you are. Here's one a few years ago, just before she died. She was all dressed up for an interview in clothes which I bought for her especially."

I held my hand out for the album, wanting to see the photo. Mrs Harris handed it over. Taking a deep breath, I slowly bent my head to look at it.

There in front of my eyes was an image of Vicky wearing ... a silver blouse and black trousers; the very ones I'd first seen her wearing when she turned up at our door.

"Oh my word!" I said.

"What's wrong, dear?" Mrs Harris said.

I replied with the only thing I could think of to say. "Do you believe in ghosts?"

Mrs Harris smiled at me, a smile just like Vicky's, the same dimple appearing in the chin and small nose wrinkling like she'd heard a joke and lighting up the face. I felt my heart calming down and my brain telling me that there was a rational explanation for all this.

Then Mrs Harris said, "Has my Vicky been to see you recently? Is that why you're here?"

I nodded, unable to speak.

"I thought she had. I smelt lavender on you, so sensed she'd been around. How has she helped you, Mrs Jameson? I know she has."

"She showed me how to get my two young children to behave better and obey me. How did you know? Apart from the lavender smell, that is."

"I've felt a restless energy in this house for the last week. Only today, it calmed down and I felt happier than I've been for years."

"She said that she lived here, but you …"

"Yes, she did. With me while she trained and started her first job."

"You said she died from drugs?"

"Yes, she got in with the wrong crowd. She had just finished training as a nanny. She wanted to help out and be like her mother. But then she met a boy who took her to a party and gave her drugs to try. She became seriously ill, went into hospital. It was hard seeing her like that, in a coma. It stole her smile. She had this smile that when she beamed at you, you felt that all was well and you would do anything for her."

"I know what you mean," I murmured. "That is sad." The truth hit me; my suspicions were right. "That means Vicky's … a ghost?"

"Doesn't it bother you that you had a ghost in the house with the children?" Mrs Harris asked.

"No. Vicky didn't mean any harm, on the contrary. Thanks to her, I can now control Sam and Jenny, and feed Robbie,." As I said this a warm feeling, like someone hugging me, wafted through me. Then I glanced at the photo I'd first seen of Vicky, and I was sure I saw the figure in it give me a thumbs-up sign.

* * *

Eileen Harris looked at the photo of her granddaughter.

"Thank you, Vicky. You heard my pleas for help to get those Jameson children to behave. You got your chance to be a nanny after all. Now you can rest in peace."

Just like I can, she thought, relishing the quietness from next door. She smiled as the photo glowed sky-blue.

Read the beginning of Book 1 of The Secrets of Singleton called 'The Snakeskin Boots'.

"Could you get that, please, Paula," Fiona Anderson called out from the hallway. "I'm must putting my coat on."

"Do I have to, Mum?" Paula muttered, getting up from the kitchen table. She walked to the phone, toast in hand.

A minute later, she shouted, "It's for you."

"Who is it?"

"Bertha Billings."

"Could you take a message for me?"

Paula jotted down the message, and returned to the table to finish her breakfast.

Her mother appeared then. "What did Bertha want?"

"She said, could you take the minutes for the meeting as Caroline has had to go to a charity event?"

"I have a better idea. How about you do the minutes? I have something I want to discuss with Bertha."

"It's my day off."

"It'll just be for today. And it'll help us out. Please, Paula."

"Okay, all right, then."

"Thanks. Bertha's an early bird, so as soon as you're ready, we'll go."

Inside the hall, Fiona said to the group standing in the centre, "Paula's agreed to take the minutes for us today."

"Good," Bertha Billings said. "Now you're here, we can start."

The eldest in the village, Bertha had lived there longer than anyone else, therefore she'd appointed herself as the chairperson.

"There are a few minor points to mention, and one major one, which we'll leave to last. Item one is the rubbish on the streets. We need to do something about that."

"I'll look into it," Ted Cooke, who owned the park cafe, said. "I'll speak to the park manager."

"Thanks, Ted. Next is the forthcoming village fete. We need to take part and have a stall again. Are you all willing to be involved?"

There was a chorus of yeses.

"That leads me to the final item, and the most important one."

"I'm thirsty," Ted said. "All this talking is making my mouth dry."

"So am I," Fiona said. "Why don't you make the refreshments, please, Paula. I'll carry on with the minutes."

Paula did as instructed. She left them to chatter and went to the kitchen. It gave her time to think about things – namely the new guy at work, Gareth Farlow. He was quite a dish, with his dark blond hair, grey eyes and easy smile. Recalling his smile, Paula frowned. He'd smiled at all the others in the office, but not at her. Why?

The low mumble of voices broke into her thoughts, and she began to wonder about the older village residents.

There was Bertha Billings. She was ninety if a day. You could tell she was in charge of the meeting by the way she stood straight as if she'd been in the army. Probably had been, Paula thought. Then there was Caroline Pritcher, who had long grey hair. It made her look ancient. She ran the local charity shop with her nephew, Archie. Next was Ted Cooke. He appeared to be eating his profits by the size of him. He must be over sixty, she reckoned. Lastly there was Daisy Roselee from the florist. Thin as a rake and her voice was weedy too, like her flowers in the shop. That voice grated on her nerves. What could Mum have to talk about to these people? Business probably, which was likely to be boring. Only one way to find out.

She crept to the door. "What do you have in mind for her, Fiona?" she heard Bertha Billings ask in her deep tone. Definitely been in the army. Were they on about her?

Paula pressed her ear to the door. If they were discussing her, she wanted to know what it was.

"I have the perfect idea how to cheer her up. And it will change her for the better," her mum said.

She squashed her ear even closer to the door. They must be whispering or talking more quietly, because she couldn't hear what was being said. Had they realised she was listening to them? The only word she could make out was 'boot'.

Chairs scraped then. She moved away from the door to the worktop. As she did, the kettle clicked off. She went to the cupboard and busied herself pouring the teas and coffees.

A minute later, the door opened to reveal her mum, smiling. "I've had an idea," she said, "I know what will cheer you up."

I doubt it, Paula thought.

"New boots. Come to my shop and choose any pair you like. I'll just go and open up. See you in there."

What was the hurry, Paula wondered. All the same, she thought about the prospect of new boots. If there was one thing she loved, it was boots. What did she fancy? Snakeskin ones.

She took the tray into the hall, kicking the door open as she went.

"Thanks, Paula," Bertha said, as she placed the tray on the table.

"I'm off to buy those new boots Mum said I could have," Paula said. "Bye."

In the shop, her mum greeted her. "Hello, Paula. You can choose whatever you like. Don't worry about paying for them. See them as a treat from me."

Paula wandered round the shop. Looked like her mum had new stock in.

As soon as she saw the knee-high patterned snakeskin boots, she knew she had to have them. She felt her heart beat loud at the sight of them. They cried out to her, Buy Us!

As her mum was busy with a customer, she decided to try on the boots herself. She went to take the pair out of the window. "Ah. I thought you might choose those. Why don't you take a seat and try them on?" her mother said, going by with several boxes.

Paula sat down on one of the seats and took off her shoes. When her mother came back empty-handed, she handed them to her. Was her mum rubbing the boots? Maybe she liked the feel of them, too.

"Let me put these on for you." Fiona bent down in front of her.

So Paula sat and watched her mum ease the boots up over her legs.

"They suit you, darling." Her mother sounded strangely pleased with herself.

"Thank you." Paula smiled, her grey eyes sparkling with happiness.

They did suit her. Her legs looked slimmer, and the heels gave her that extra lift. When she saw the boots properly in the mirror, she could see the pattern on them clearly. She peered at the reflection. Yes. Definitely a pattern, which looked like snakes, but on closer inspection was Ss up and down the leather. Wow! She bet no one else had boots like these.

Paula twirled around, admiring her reflection from one angle, then another, so that her brown bob-styled hair swished around her face. The boots made her feel a different person. Instead of the heavy feeling in her heart, she had a warm sensation like the sun rising in her. She stood up straighter.

"I'll have them," she said.

As Paula left the shop, the door slammed shut behind her. She pulled her hand away fast before her fingers were trapped. She frowned. There was no one by the door; her mum was at the counter. There was no breeze, either. It felt as though the shop wanted her to leave. But she quickly forgot about this and smiled at the thought of what the others would say about her new boots.

Acknowledgements

I would like to thank:

Dr Hilary Johnson for her edits and comments, which once again have made me think about what I am writing. I will keep these in mind for the rest of the series.

Joleene Naylor for the fab cover and helping make this into a new brand for me.

To the Writers Guide to Epublishing group who beta-read the original story when I first wrote it six years ago.

About the author:

I live in SE London. I am an indie author of adult magical realism and ghost stories and children's magical realism. I also write magazine fillers. I blog about my writing life, and my Asperger's Syndrome.

Do I believe in ghosts and/or the afterlife? I don't know, to be honest. I would have said no before, but there must be something inside me that does sort of belief in some thing because I have written YA ebooks about teenage guardian angels, the Geraldine's Gems series about a lady who returns to help her living relatives and there are ghosts that appear in the Singleton series. And now there is this new series of short stories about ghosts helping families in crisis. So, I will leave you to work that one out.

A message from Julie

Thank you for buying and reading this ebook. If you liked it enough, please could you post a review on the website you bought it from. Thank you. Also, if you would like to know when my next book or event is, why not sign up to my newsletter at http://eepurl.com/b3zDYv

Connect with Me Online
  Twitter: http://www.twitter.com/@juliedayauthor
  Facebook: http://facebook.com/JulieDay
  My website: http://www.julieaday.co.uk
  My blog: http://www.julieaday.blogspot.com
  Other books by Julie Day

For adults (magical realism): Geraldine's Gems series
  One Good Turn
  More Fish in the Sea
  A Trouble Shared
  Don't Get Mad
  Life in the Old Dog
  A Friend In Need
  Birds Flock Together
  The Secrets of Singleton
  The Snakeskin Boots
  The Cameo Brooch
  The Chocolate Cupcake

Printed in Great Britain
by Amazon